ANIMAL
ADVENTURES

The Little House
Chapter Book Collection

The Adventures of Laura & Jack
Pioneer Sisters
Animal Adventures
School Days
Laura & Nellie
Christmas Stories

ANIMAL ADVENTURES

ADAPTED FROM THE **LITTLE HOUSE** BOOKS BY

Laura Ingalls Wilder

Illustrated by Ji-Hyuk Kim

HARPER

An Imprint of HarperCollinsPublishers

Adaptation by Melissa Peterson

Little House® is a trademark of
HarperCollins Publishers Inc.

Animal Adventures
Text adapted from *Little House on the Prairie*, copyright 1935, 1963, Little House
Heritage Trust; *Little House in the Big Woods*, copyright 1932, 1960, Little House
Heritage Trust; *On the Banks of Plum Creek*, copyright 1937, 1965, Little House
Heritage Trust; *By the Shores of Silver Lake*, copyright 1939, 1967, Little House
Heritage Trust.
Text copyright © 1997 by HarperCollins Publishers
Illustrations by Ji-Hyuk Kim

Library of Congress Control Number: 2016941456
ISBN 978-0-06-237712-8

Typography by Jenna Stempel
21 BRR 10 9 8 7 6 5 4
❖
Revised edition, 2017

Contents

CHAPTER 1
TWO BEARS IN
THE BIG WOODS

The Big Woods were full of wolves and panthers. Gray foxes had dens in the hills. White-tailed deer roamed among the trees. There were even bears in the woods. Once Laura saw one up close, though she didn't know it at the time.

It happened when Laura was small. Her sister Mary was a bit older, and Carrie was just a baby. They lived in a little log house with Pa and Ma, a bulldog named Jack and a cat named Black Susan.

Spring had just begun to come to the woods. Early one morning Pa said he must go to town. He tied up a bundle of his furs to trade. There were so many furs that the bundle was almost as big as Pa. With so much to carry he had to leave his gun at home.

Ma was worried. But Pa said he would walk very fast and be home before dark.

The nearest town was far away. Laura and Mary knew Pa would bring them home presents from the store. All day long they waited.

Finally the sun sank low above the treetops. Laura and Mary watched eagerly for Pa. Then the sun sank out of sight, and still he did not come.

The woods grew dark. Ma started supper and set the table. But still Pa did not come.

Soon it was time to do the chores. Ma said

Laura could come with her while she milked the cow. Laura could carry the lantern. Laura was proud to be helping Ma. She held the lantern carefully. Little bits of light leaped around her on the snow. Night had almost come. There was just a dim gray light in the dark woods.

Laura saw the shape of Sukey, the brown cow, standing at the barnyard gate. She was surprised. So was Ma. It was too early in the spring for Sukey to be let out in the woods to eat grass. Why wasn't she in the barn?

But Laura remembered that sometimes Pa left Sukey's stall door open so she could come into the barnyard. Maybe that was why she was out.

Ma pushed against the gate to open it, but Sukey was standing against it. The gate wouldn't open.

"Sukey!" Ma said. "Get over!" She reached

across the gate and slapped Sukey's big shoulder.

Just then a bit of light from the lantern shone on Sukey. Laura saw long, shaggy black fur. She saw two little, glittering eyes.

Sukey had short brown fur and large, gentle eyes.

Ma said, very quietly, "Laura, walk back to the house."

So Laura turned around and began to walk. Ma came behind her. Halfway there Ma snatched Laura up, lantern and all, and ran. She raced into the house and slammed the door.

"Ma," Laura said, "was it a bear?"

"Yes, Laura," Ma said. "It was a bear."

Laura began to cry. She hung on to Ma and sobbed, "Oh, will he eat Sukey?"

Ma hugged her. "No, Sukey is safe in the barn. The door is made to keep bears out.

The bear cannot get in."

Laura felt better. "But he could have hurt us, couldn't he?" she asked.

"He didn't hurt us," Ma said. "You were a good girl, Laura, to do exactly as I told you, without asking why."

Ma was trembling. Suddenly she laughed. "To think I've slapped a bear!"

Then she put supper on the table for Laura and Mary. Pa still had not come home.

After supper Laura and Mary put on their nightgowns. They said their prayers. Ma sat by the lamp mending one of Pa's shirts while Laura and Mary snuggled into their trundle bed.

Without Pa, the house seemed cold and still and strange. Laura listened to the wind in the Big Woods. It went crying around the house as though it were lost in the dark and the cold.

Ma finished mending the shirt. Then Laura saw her do something Ma had never done before. She went to the door and pulled the latch-string through its hole. Now no one could get inside unless Ma lifted the latch.

Ma went to the big bed and took out Carrie, all limp and sleeping. She took her to the rocking chair and sat there rocking gently. When Laura and Mary fell asleep, she was still sitting there rocking. Pa had not come home.

But in the morning, there he was! He had brought candy for Laura and Mary and pretty calico for new dresses. And he had brought home a story—another bear story.

It had taken Pa a long time to do the trading yesterday. "It was nearly sundown before I could start home," he said. "I tried to hurry, but the walking was hard and I was tired. I had not gone far before night came.

And I was alone in the Big Woods without my gun."

Laura and Mary looked at Pa with wide, scared eyes.

Pa went on. "I knew that some of the bears had come out of their dens. I had seen their tracks when I went to town in the morning. Bears are hungry and cross at this time of year. I did not want to meet one.

"Then I came into an open place, and there, right in the middle of the road, I saw a big black bear."

Laura gasped. Mary's mouth was a round, scared O. "He was standing up on his hind legs," said Pa, "looking at me. I could see his eyes shine. I could see his pig snout. I could even see one of his claws in the starlight.

"My scalp prickled and my hair stood straight up. I stopped in my tracks. The bear didn't move. There he stood, looking at me.

"I knew it would do no good to try to go around him. He would follow me into the dark woods, where he could see better than I. I had to pass that bear to get home."

Laura's heart was thumping inside her. Pa went on. "I thought that if I could scare him, he might get out of the road and let me go by. So I took a deep breath, and suddenly I shouted with all my might and ran at him, waving my arms.

"He didn't move.

"I stopped and looked at him, and he stood looking at me. Then I shouted again. There he stood. I kept on shouting and waving my arms, but he did not budge.

"At last I looked around, and I got a good big club, a solid, heavy branch. I lifted it up in my hands, and I ran straight at that bear. I swung my club as hard as I could and brought it down, *bang!* on his head.

"And there he still stood, for he was nothing but a big, black, burned stump!"

"It wasn't really a bear at all?" Mary asked.

"No, Mary, it wasn't a bear at all," Pa laughed. "There I had been yelling, and dancing, and waving my arms, all by myself in the Big Woods, trying to scare a stump!"

"Ours was really a bear," Laura said. "But we weren't scared, because we thought it was Sukey."

Pa did not say anything, but he hugged her tight.

Laura snuggled closer to him. "That bear might have eaten Ma and me all up! But Ma walked right up to him and slapped him, and he didn't do anything. Why didn't he do anything?"

"I guess he was too surprised to do anything, Laura," Pa said. "I guess he was afraid when the lantern shone in his eyes.

And when Ma walked up to him and slapped him, he knew she wasn't afraid."

"Well, you were brave, too," Laura said. "Even if it was only a stump, you thought it was a bear."

CHAPTER 2

GRANDPA AND THE PANTHER

One winter night, Pa looked at Black Susan, the cat, stretching herself before the fire. He said to Laura, "Do you know that a panther is a cat? A great big wild cat?"

"No," said Laura.

"Well, it is," said Pa. "Just imagine Black Susan bigger than Jack, and fiercer than Jack when he growls. Then she would be just like a panther."

He settled Laura and Mary on his knees.

"I'll tell you about Grandpa and the panther," he said.

"Your Grandpa?" Laura asked.

"No, Laura, your Grandpa. My father."

"Oh," said Laura. She wriggled closer against Pa's arm. She knew her Grandpa. He lived far away in the Big Woods, in a big log house.

"Your Grandpa went to town one day," Pa began. "He was late starting home. It was dark when he came riding his horse through the Big Woods. He could hardly see the road.

"He heard a panther scream. He was frightened, for he had no gun."

"How does a panther scream?" Laura asked.

"Like this," Pa said. And he screamed a loud, horrible scream. Mary and Laura shivered with terror. Even Ma jumped in her chair.

"Mercy, Charles!" she said.

But Mary and Laura loved to be scared like that.

Pa went on. "Grandpa's horse ran fast, for it was frightened too. But it could not get away from the panther.

It was a hungry panther. It moved as fast as the horse could run. It screamed on one side of the road. Then it screamed on the other side. It was always close behind.

"Grandpa leaned forward in the saddle. He nudged the horse to run faster. The horse was running as fast as it could. Still the panther screamed close behind.

"Then Grandpa caught a glimpse of it as it leaped from treetop to treetop. It was a huge, black panther, leaping through the air like Black Susan leaping on a mouse. It was many, many times bigger than Black Susan. If it leaped on Grandpa it could kill him with its slashing claws and long, sharp teeth.

"Grandpa, on his horse, was running away from it just as a mouse runs from a cat.

"The panther did not scream anymore. Grandpa did not see it anymore. But he knew it was coming. The horse ran as fast as it could.

"At last Grandpa reached his house. He jumped off the horse and burst through the door and slammed it behind him. The panther landed on the horse's back. It landed just where Grandpa had been.

"The horse screamed and ran away toward the Big Woods, with the panther ripping his back with its claws. But Grandpa grabbed his gun and got to the window just in time to shoot the panther dead.

"Grandpa said," Pa finished, "that never

15

again would he go into the Big Woods without his gun."

Laura and Mary shivered and snuggled closer to Pa. They were safe and snug on his knees, with his strong arms around them.

CHAPTER 3
LOOKING FOR A DEER

One night Pa said he would go to his deer lick in the woods and watch for a deer. A deer lick was a place where the deer came to get salt. Pa had made it by sprinkling salt over the ground. It was in an open place in the woods, with trees nearby for Pa to sit in.

After supper Pa took his gun and went into the woods. That night Laura and Mary had to go to sleep without any stories or music.

In the morning there was no deer hanging from the tree.

Laura and Mary did not know what to think. Pa had never before gone out to get a deer and come home without one.

Pa worked hard outside all day, so Mary and Laura had to wait until after supper to find out why he hadn't come home with a deer.

After they had finished eating, Pa took Laura on his knee. Mary sat close by in her little chair. "Now," said Pa, "I'll tell you why you had no fresh meat to eat today.

"I went out to the deer lick. I climbed up into a big oak tree. I was near enough to shoot any animal that came to it, and my gun was loaded.

"I was a little tired from chopping wood all day yesterday, and I must have fallen asleep.

When I opened my eyes, the big, round moon was just rising. I could see it between the bare branches of the trees. And right against it I saw a deer standing.

"His head was up and he was listening. His great, branching horns stood out above his head. He was dark against the moon.

"It was a perfect shot. But he was so beautiful, he looked so strong and free and wild, that I couldn't kill him. I sat there and looked at him, until he bounded away into the dark woods.

"Then I remembered that Ma and my little girls were waiting for me to bring home some good fresh venison. I made up my mind that next time I would shoot.

"After a while a big bear came lumbering out into the open. He was so fat from feasting on berries and roots and grubs all summer

20

that he was nearly as large as two bears. His head swayed from side to side as he went on all fours across the clear space in the moonlight, until he came to a rotten log. He smelled it, and listened. Then he pawed it apart and sniffed among the broken pieces, eating up the fat, white grubs.

"Then he stood on his hind legs, perfectly still, looking all around him. He seemed to be suspicious that something was wrong. He was trying to see or smell what it was.

"He was a perfect mark to shoot at. But I was so much interested in watching him, and the woods were so peaceful in the moonlight, that I forgot all about my gun. I did not even think of shooting him, until he was waddling away into the woods.

"'This will never do,' I thought. 'I'll never get any meat this way.'

"I settled myself in the tree and waited again. This time I was determined to shoot the next game I saw.

"The moon had risen higher and the moonlight was bright in the little open place. All around it the shadows were dark among the trees.

"After a long while, a doe and her yearling fawn came stepping daintily out of the shadows. They were not afraid at all. They walked over to the place where I had sprinkled the salt, and they both licked up a little of it.

"Then they raised their heads and looked at each other. The fawn stepped over and stood beside the doe. They stood there together, looking at the woods and the moonlight. Their large eyes were shining and soft.

"I just sat there looking at them, until they walked away among the shadows. Then

I climbed down out of the tree and came home."

That was the end of the story. Pa looked at Laura and Mary.

"I'm *glad* you didn't shoot them!" Laura said.

Mary agreed.

CHAPTER 4
WOLVES

Early one spring, Laura's family loaded up a covered wagon. They left the Big Woods far behind. Pa built a house on the Kansas prairie, where there were hardly any trees at all.

One afternoon, Pa rode off on his horse, Patty, to see what he could see. There was plenty of meat in the house, so he didn't take his gun.

All that day Jack acted strange. He walked

up and down, looking worried. He wrinkled his nose at the wind. The hair on his neck stood on end.

"What's the matter with Jack?" Laura asked Ma.

Jack looked up at Ma, but he couldn't say anything. Ma gazed across the waving prairie grass all around them. She didn't see anything unusual.

"Likely it isn't anything, Laura," she said.

But toward nightfall Patty appeared, running hard. Pa was leaning almost flat on her neck. Patty's black coat was streaked with sweat and foam. Pa would never ride a horse so hard unless something was wrong.

"What's the matter, Charles?" Ma called.

Pa breathed a long breath. "I was afraid the wolves would beat me here. But I see everything's all right," he said.

"Wolves!" Ma cried. "What wolves?"

"Everything's all right, Caroline," said Pa. But he had a frightening story to tell.

"Fifty wolves, Caroline. The biggest wolves I ever saw!"

The sun had gone down, and a shadow came over the prairie. Pa said, "I'll tell you about it later."

Pa let Pet and Patty drink from Ma's washtub, which was ready for the next morning's washing. He didn't want to risk taking them down to the creek like he usually did. He rubbed down Patty's sweaty sides and legs and put the horses in the barn.

Supper was ready. Laura and Mary stayed close to the campfire, with Baby Carrie beside them. They ate corncakes and prairie hen while the fire flickered in the dark.

Jack sat beside Laura. He pricked his ears, listening. The hair lay flat on his thick neck, and he didn't growl. That meant everything was all right. His teeth showed a little, but that was because he was a bulldog.

Laura and Mary listened while Pa told Ma about the wolves.

As Pa was loping home on Patty, a pack of wolves had appeared out of a little hollow. They were all around Pa in a second.

"It was a big pack," Pa said. "Fifty wolves— the biggest ones I ever saw in my life. Must be what they call buffalo wolves. The leader stood three feet at the shoulder! I tell you my hair stood straight on end."

"And you didn't have your gun!" Ma said.

"I thought of that. But my gun would have been no use if I'd had it. You can't fight fifty wolves with one gun. And Patty couldn't outrun them."

"What did you do?" Ma asked.

"Nothing. Patty tried to run," Pa said. "But I knew if she even started, those wolves would be on us in a minute, pulling us down. So I held her to a walk."

"Goodness, Charles!" Ma gasped.

But the wolves hadn't paid any attention to Pa. "They must have just made a kill and eaten all they could," he said.

The wolves had trotted along beside Pa and Patty, jumping and playing like a pack of dogs. Finally they turned aside and headed down a path toward the creek. As soon as they were gone, Pa let Patty go.

"She headed straight for home, across the prairie. She couldn't have run faster if I'd been cutting into her with a rawhide whip."

Pa had worried that the wolves might be heading for the house. But they were nowhere to be seen. "All's well that ends well," Pa said. "Those wolves are miles from here by now."

Jack walked around the campfire. He stood still to smell the air and listen. Once more the hair rose on his neck.

Ma said it was bedtime for little girls. Not even Baby Carrie was sleepy yet, but Ma took them all into the house.

Laura lay in her little bed wide awake. She could smell Pa's tobacco smoke coming in from outside. After a long time, Ma and Pa came in and very quietly went to bed. But still Laura couldn't sleep.

She strained her eyes in the dark to watch Jack. He lay across the doorway, but there was no door. Pa hadn't had time to build one yet. There was only a quilt hung across the open space.

Laura couldn't tell if the hair was still standing up on Jack's neck, but she could see that his chin wasn't resting on his paws. His head was up, listening.

Suddenly she was sitting straight up in bed. She had been asleep. Pa stood in the moonlight at the window. He had his gun.

Right in Laura's ear a wolf howled.

She scooted away from the wall. The wolf was on the other side of it. Laura was too scared to make a sound.

At the doorway, Jack growled and bared his teeth.

"Be still, Jack," Pa said.

Terrible howls curled around the house. Laura rose out of bed. Pa turned to look at her.

"Want to see them, Laura?" he whispered.

Laura nodded. Pa leaned his gun against the wall and lifted her up to the window.

There beneath the moon sat a half circle of wolves. They looked at Laura in the window, and she looked at them. She had never seen such big wolves.

The biggest wolf was taller than she was. Everything about him was big—his pointed ears, his mouth with the tongue hanging out, his two front paws side by side. His coat was shaggy gray and his eyes were glittering green.

"He's awful big," Laura whispered.

"Yes, and see how his coat shines," Pa said softly. The moonlight made little glitters in the edges of the shaggy fur.

"They're in a ring clear around the house," Pa whispered. He and Laura moved to the other window. There, sure enough, was the other half of the circle of wolves. Laura could hear their breathing.

Pa went back to the first window. Laura followed him. They were just in time to see the big wolf lift his nose till it pointed straight at the sky. He gave a long, wailing howl at the moon.

All around the house the circle of wolves pointed their noses at the sky and answered

him. Their howls shuddered through the house.

"Now go back to bed, little half-pint," Pa said. "Jack and I will take care of you all."

Laura crawled back in bed. But for a long time she did not sleep. She listened to the breathing of the wolves on the other side of the wall. She could hear their claws scratching the ground. A nose snuffled at a crack in the log wall.

The big gray leader howled again, and the others answered him.

Jack never stopped pacing up and down before the quilt that hung in the doorway. He didn't like those wolves. He showed them his sharp, fierce teeth.

They could howl all they wanted, but Jack and Pa would not let them in.

CHAPTER 5
TEXAS LONGHORNS

One spring evening Laura and Pa were sitting on the doorstep. The moon shone over the dark prairie. Pa was softly playing his fiddle when Laura heard a strange sound in the distance.

"What's that!" she said.

Pa listened. "Cattle, by George!" he said. "Must be the cattle herds going north to Fort Dodge."

The next morning Laura saw two strange

men sitting on horses by the stable. They were talking to Pa. The men were brown from the sun and their eyes were narrow slits between squinting eyelids. They wore flaps of leather over their legs, handkerchiefs knotted around their necks, and wide-brimmed hats.

"So long," they said to Pa. "Hi! Yip!" they said to their horses, and they galloped away.

"Here's a piece of luck!" Pa told Ma. Those men were cowboys. They wanted Pa to help them herd their cattle past the creek bluffs. Pa wouldn't charge them any money, but, "How would you like a good piece of beef?" he asked Ma.

"Oh, Charles!" said Ma. Her eyes shone. They never had beef to eat, just prairie hen and jackrabbit.

Pa tied a big handkerchief around his neck. He showed Laura how he could pull it over his mouth and nose to keep the dust out.

Then he rode away on his horse to join the cowboys.

All that day Laura and Mary could hear the sound of the cattle herds coming nearer. It was a faint, mournful sound of cattle mooing.

At noon dust was blowing along the horizon. Ma said that all those cattle trampled the grasses flat and stirred up a cloud of dust.

At sunset, Pa came riding home, covered with dust. There was dust in his beard and dust in his hair and dust puffing off his clothes. He did not bring any beef, because the cattle weren't across the creek yet.

That night Pa went to bed soon after supper. Laura lay awake, listening to the cowboys singing away out on the prairie. Their songs were high, lonely, wailing songs, almost like wolves howling.

Laura could hear the cattle mooing softly, and sometimes real wolves howled far, far away. But mostly she heard the cowboys' songs rising and falling and wailing away.

When everyone else was asleep, Laura crept to the window. She could see three fires gleaming like red eyes way out on the prairie. The sky was big and still and full of moonlight. The lonely songs seemed to be crying for the moon. They made Laura's throat ache.

All the next day Laura and Mary watched toward the west. They could hear the far-away bawling of the cattle. They could see the dust blowing.

Suddenly a dozen cattle appeared on the prairie, not far from the stable. They had long, sharp horns. Their tails stood up and their feet pounded the ground.

A cowboy on a spotted horse galloped madly to get in front of them. He waved his big hat and yelled sharp, high yells.

"Hi! Yi-yi-yi! Hi!" yelled the cowboy.

The cattle turned, clashing their long horns together. They galloped away, tails held high. The cowboy's horse raced after them, herding them together. They all went over a rise of ground and down out of sight.

Laura ran back and forth, waving her sunbonnet. "Hi! Yi-yi-yi!" she yelled, until Ma told her to stop. Laura wished she could be a cowboy.

Late that afternoon three riders came out of the west. A lone cow came with them. One of the riders was Pa, on Patty. Slowly they came nearer, and soon Laura could see a little spotted calf alongside the cow. The cow mooed loudly and the little calf bleated.

Two cowboys held ropes tied around the cow's horns. They rode up to the stable and held the ropes while Pa tied up the cow to the stable wall. Then the cowboys said good-bye and rode away.

A cow! Ma could not believe it. Now they could have milk to drink! The calf was too small to travel, Pa said, and the cow would be too thin to sell. So the cowboys had given them to Pa. There was also a big chunk of beef tied to Pa's saddle.

Pa and Ma and Mary and Laura and even Baby Carrie laughed for joy. Pa's laugh was like great bells ringing. Ma's smile made Laura feel warm all over.

"Give me the bucket, Caroline," said Pa. He was going to milk the cow right away.

He took the bucket and squatted by the cow. And that cow hunched herself and kicked Pa flat on his face.

Pa jumped up. His face was blazing red and his eyes snapped blue sparks.

"Now, by the Great Horn Spoon, I'll milk her!" he said.

He got his ax and he sharpened two thick

slabs of oak. He pushed the cow against the stable and drove the slabs deep into the ground beside her. The cow bawled and the little calf squalled.

Pa tied poles firmly to the posts to make a fence. Now the cow could not move forward or backward or sideways. But the little calf could nudge its way between its mother and the stable. Then it felt safe and stopped its squalling. It stood on that side of the cow and drank its supper, and Pa put his hand through the fence and milked from the other side. He got a tin cup almost full of milk.

"We'll try again in the morning," he said. "The poor thing's as wild as a deer. But we'll gentle her, we'll gentle her."

Mary and Laura told Pa to give the cup of milk to Baby Carrie. They watched her drink it. The tin cup hid Carrie's small face. But

Laura could see gulps of milk going down her throat.

Gulp by gulp, Carrie swallowed all that good milk. Then she licked the foam from her lips and laughed.

For dinner that night there were sizzling beef steaks. Nothing had ever tasted so good as that tough, juicy beef. Everyone was happy, because now there would be milk for all of them to drink, and maybe even butter for their cornbread.

The lowing of the cattle herds was far away again. Across the prairie floated the cowboys' songs, almost too faint to be heard.

CHAPTER 6
OLD GRAY BADGER

For a time Laura and her family lived near a little creek. It was called Plum Creek, and it ran swift and clear across the Minnesota prairie. In one place, a short walk from Laura's house, the creek widened into a deep pool.

Sometimes Pa took Mary and Laura swimming in the pool. If they splashed too far into the deep end of the pool, Pa ducked them under the water. It was scary to be ducked, but lots of fun too.

Pa warned Laura and Mary to stay away from the deep water. "Don't you ever go near that swimming hole unless I am with you," he said. The water was too deep for little girls to play in by themselves.

One day the hot sun beat down on Laura as she played on the prairie. Pa was away, and Mary stayed in the dugout with Ma. Laura wandered through the tall grasses alone. The wind was scorching and smothery. Laura grew terribly thirsty.

The dugout was far away, but the cool water of the swimming hole was very near. Laura knew she must not go near the pool. She remembered Pa's warning. She must stay away. She mustn't go near that water. That clear, deep, shady water.

Suddenly she turned around and hurried

toward it. She'd just take a look at it, she thought. Just looking at the water would make her feel better.

Then she had a better idea. She could wade in the edge of the water, just to cool her feet. She wouldn't go anywhere near the deep water. She trotted faster toward the pool.

Halfway down the path she stopped short. There was an animal standing right in the middle of the path.

Laura jumped back and stared. She had never seen such an animal. It was almost as long as Jack. But its legs were shorter than Jack's. Long gray fur bristled all over it. It had a flat head and small ears. Its flat head slowly tilted up and stared at Laura.

She stared back at its funny face. And while they stood still and staring, the animal did a very strange thing.

It widened and shortened and spread flat

on the ground. It grew flatter and flatter, till it looked just like a gray fur lying on the dirt. It was not like a real animal at all, except for the eyes staring up at Laura.

Slowly and carefully, Laura stooped to the ground. She picked up a willow stick. That made her feel better. She stayed bent over, looking at that flat gray fur.

It didn't move. Neither did Laura.

Laura wondered what would happen if she poked it. Maybe it would change to some other shape.

Gently she poked it with the short stick.

The gray fur let out a frightful snarl. Its eyes glittered, and it snapped at Laura with fierce white teeth. Its teeth snapped shut almost on Laura's nose.

Laura ran with all her might. She could run fast. She didn't stop running until she was back at the dugout.

"Goodness, Laura!" Ma said. "You'll make yourself sick, tearing around so in this heat."

Laura had been bad and she knew it. She had broken her promise to Pa. But no one had seen her. Except for that strange animal, and it couldn't tell.

But Laura felt worse and worse inside. Breaking a promise was as bad as telling a lie. Laura wished she hadn't done it. But she had, and if Pa knew, he would punish her.

That night she lay awake beside Mary. Pa sat outside the door, playing his fiddle in the starlight. Everything was beautiful and good, except Laura.

Pa's fiddle sang to her sweetly. Pa thought she was a good little girl.

At last Laura could bear it no longer.

She slid out of bed and tiptoed to the door. She stood beside Pa in her white nightgown. Pa smiled down at her.

"What is it, little half-pint?" he asked her. "You look like a little ghost, all white in the dark."

"Pa," Laura said, in a quivery small voice, "I—I—started to go to the swimming hole."

"You did!" Pa exclaimed. Then he asked, "Well, what stopped you?"

"I don't know," Laura whispered. "It had gray fur and it—it flattened out flat. It snarled."

"How big was it?" Pa asked.

Laura told him all about the strange animal.

"It must have been a badger," Pa said.

Then for a long time he did not say anything else. Laura waited.

"Well," he said at last. "I hardly know what to do, Laura. You see, I trusted you. Do you know what people have to do to anyone they can't trust?"

"What?" Laura whispered.

"They have to watch him," said Pa. "So I guess you must be watched. Tomorrow you stay where Ma can watch you. You are not to go out of her sight all day. If you are good all day, then we will let you try again to be a girl we can trust."

The next day was a dreadful day.

Ma was mending, and Laura had to stay in the dugout. She could not even fetch water from the spring, for that was out of Ma's sight.

Mary fetched the water. Mary took Carrie to walk on the prairie. Laura had to stay in.

Jack laid his nose on his paws and wagged his tail, begging Laura to come out. He couldn't understand why she did not.

Laura helped Ma. She washed the dishes and made the beds. She swept the floor and set the table. After the noon meal she washed the dishes again. Then she hemmed a sheet for Ma. Over and over she made tiny stitches in the seam.

Laura thought that seam and that day would never end.

But at last Ma said it was time for supper.

"You have been a good girl, Laura," Ma said. "We will tell Pa so. And tomorrow morning you and I are going to look for that badger. I am sure he saved you from drowning, for if you had gone to that deep water you would have gone into it. Once you begin being naughty, it is easier to go on and on, and sooner or later something dreadful happens."

"Yes, Ma," said Laura. She knew that now.

The whole day was gone. Laura had missed a whole day of cloud-shadows on the prairie and water bugs skating on the creek.

She was sure that being good could never be as hard as being watched.

The next day she went with Ma to look for the badger. She showed Ma the place where he had flattened himself on the grass.

Ma found the hole where the badger lived. It was a round hole under a clump of grass on the prairie bank. Laura called to him and poked a stick into the hole.

If the badger was at home, he would not come out. Laura never saw that old gray badger again.

CHAPTER 7
THE BLACK PONIES

Once, when Laura was getting to be a big girl, her family visited Ma's sister. Aunt Docia and her family lived at a railroad camp where men were working to build a railroad.

It was dark when Pa drove the wagon up to Aunt Docia's log shanty house. She stood smiling in the doorway. "Come right in!" she called. "Supper's waiting!"

Inside the warm house a lamp gave off a soft glow. Aunt Docia said, "Well, Lena and

Jean, aren't you going to say anything to your cousins?"

"How do you do?" Lena said. She was a year older than Laura. Her eyes were black and snappy. Her curly hair was black as black could be. Laura liked her.

"How do you do?" said Laura and Mary and Carrie. Carrie wasn't a baby any longer.

Jean didn't say anything at all. But Lena smiled. "Do you like to ride horseback?" she asked Laura. "We've got two black ponies. Tomorrow I'm going for the washing and you can come too, if you want to. Do you?"

"Yes!" said Laura.

That night Laura slept in a tent with Lena. The little house was too crowded with Pa and Ma and Mary and Carrie and Uncle Hi and Aunt Docia and cousin Jean.

The next morning Lena jumped up bright and early. "Hurry up!" she sang out. "We're going for the washing!"

Laura ran outside behind her. The wide prairie stretched out beneath a sunny sky. Laura saw two black ponies grazing in the tall prairie grass. Their shining manes and tails were blowing in the wind.

"We've got to eat breakfast first," Lena said. "Come on, Laura! Hurry!" They raced to the house where everyone else was already at the table.

Breakfast was jolly. Pa's great laugh rang out like bells. Afterward Laura helped Lena carry a harness to Uncle Hi's buggy.

Uncle Hi worked at the railroad camp, and Aunt Docia did the cooking for all the other railroad men. There were so many meals to cook, and so many dishes to wash that Aunt Docia and Lena were busy from sunrise to sunset every day.

There was never any time for them to

wash their clothes. Aunt Docia had hired a homesteader's wife to do it for her. The homesteader lived three miles away. It was Lena's job to drive the buggy to pick up the washing.

Lena untied the black ponies from their picket lines. Laura helped her harness them to the buggy. Lena climbed into the buggy, and Laura climbed up next to her. Lena took the reins.

Pa had never let Laura drive his horses. He said she wasn't strong enough to hold them if they ran away.

As soon as Lena took the reins, the black ponies began to trot. The prairie wind blew into their faces. The buggy wheels turned swiftly. Faster and faster went the ponies. Laura and Lena laughed with joy.

The trotting ponies touched noses, gave a little squeal, and began to run.

Up sailed the buggy. Laura was almost bounced off the seat. Her bonnet flapped behind her. The ponies were stretched out low, running with all their might.

"They're running away!" Laura cried out.

"Let 'em run!" Lena shouted. "They can't run against anything but grass! Hi! Yi, yee-ee!" she yelled at the ponies.

Their long black manes and tails streamed on the wind. Their feet pounded. The buggy sailed. Everything went rushing by too fast to be seen.

"Hi, yi, yi, yi, yipee-ee!" yelled Lena and Laura. But the ponies couldn't go any faster. They were running as fast as they could.

"I guess I better breathe them," Lena said. She pulled at the lines till she made the ponies trot. After a bit they slowed to a walk. Everything seemed quiet and slow.

"I wish I could drive," Laura said. "I always

wanted to, but Pa won't let me."

"You can drive a ways," Lena offered.

Just then the ponies touched noses again, squealed, and ran.

"You can drive on the way home!" Lena promised.

Singing and whooping, they went racing on across the prairie. Every time Lena slowed the ponies to get their breath, they got it and ran again. In no time at all, they reached the homesteader's little one-room shack.

The homesteader's wife came out to the buggy. She carried a heavy basket of washing. Her face and arms and bare feet were brown as leather from the sun. Lena put the washing into the back of the buggy. Before long Lena and Laura had left the little shack far behind. They drove slowly for a while, talking.

Then Laura asked, "May I drive now?"

Lena handed her the lines. "All you have

to do is hold the lines," she said. "The ponies know the way back."

At that instant, the ponies touched noses and squealed.

"Hold on to them, Laura! Hold on to them!" Lena screeched.

Laura braced her feet and hung on to the lines with all her might. She could feel that the ponies didn't mean any harm. They were running because they wanted to run.

Laura hung on to them. "Yi, yi, yi, yipee!" she yelled.

She had forgotten the basket of clothes. So had Lena.

All the way back across the prairie they went whooping and singing. The ponies ran, then trotted, then ran again.

All too soon they reached the railroad camp. Laura and Lena began to climb out of the buggy. Then they saw that the clean clothes had spilled out and fell under the seats.

Guiltily they picked up the clothes. They smoothed them out as best they could. Together they lugged the heavy basket into the shanty. Ma and Aunt Docia were there, dishing up dinner.

"Your girls look as if butter wouldn't melt in your mouths," said Aunt Docia. "What have you been up to?"

"Why, we just drove out and brought back the washing," said Lena.

It was their secret.

CHAPTER 8
THE WOLVES' DEN

One winter Laura's family stayed in a big house near Silver Lake on the Dakota prairie. The house belonged to some surveyors. Pa agreed to watch it during the winter, while he searched for a homestead.

The surveyors left to go back east. Laura and her family were the only people for miles around. It was a cold, cold winter.

One night Laura looked out the window. The moonlight shone silver clear. The earth was endless white, and the wind was still.

Laura felt restless. Pa was playing his fiddle, but Laura hardly noticed the music. She didn't want to dance. The white frosty world called to her.

"Carrie!" she exclaimed suddenly. "Let's go slide on the ice!"

"In the night, Laura?" Ma was surprised.

"It's light outdoors," Laura said. "Almost as light as day."

"It will be all right, Caroline," said Pa. "There's nothing to hurt them, if they don't stay too long and freeze."

So Ma said they might go. Laura and Carrie hurried into their coats. They put on their hoods and mittens and scarves. They wore warm flannel petticoats beneath their wool dresses.

They burst out of the warm house. The cold air took their breath away. Laura raced

Carrie down the snowy path to the lake.

They walked out onto the frozen lake. The great round moon hung in the sky above them. All around them was the cold, still dark. Behind them yellow lights twinkled from the windows of the house.

"How still it is," Carrie whispered. "Listen."

Laura's heart swelled. She felt like she was part of the land and the sky and the moonlight. She wanted to fly.

But Carrie was little and almost afraid. Laura took her hand and said, "Let's slide. Come on, run!"

With hands clasped, they ran a little way. Then they stopped running and slid. They could slide a long way with each run.

The moon's light made a silver path on the ice.

"On the moon path, Carrie!" Laura cried.

"Let's follow the moon path!"

And so they ran and slid on the glittering moon path. They ran and slid, and ran and slid, again and again. They went farther and farther from the shore.

They swooped and almost seemed to fly. If Carrie lost her balance, Laura held her up. Sometimes Laura wobbled, and Carrie's hand steadied her.

They slid clear across the lake, almost to the other shore. Suddenly they stopped. Something made Laura look up to the top of the bank.

There, dark against the moonlight, stood a great big wolf.

He was looking right at Laura. The wind ruffled his fur.

"Let's go back," Laura said quickly. She turned Carrie around. "I can go faster than you."

She ran and slid and ran again as fast as she could. Carrie kept up.

"I saw it too," Carrie said. "Was it a wolf?"

"Don't talk!" Laura answered. "Hurry!"

They ran and slid. Laura could hear their feet hitting the ice. She listened for a sound behind them. Nothing.

Finally they reached the path at the edge of the lake. They ran up the path. Laura looked back, but she couldn't see anything.

They kept right on running, up the path to the house and through the door.

Laura slammed the door shut behind them. She leaned against the door, panting.

"What is it?" said Pa, jumping to his feet. "What has frightened you?"

"Was it a wolf, Laura?" Carrie gasped.

"It was a wolf, Pa," Laura gulped. She could hardly catch her breath. "A great big wolf! I was afraid Carrie couldn't run fast enough but she did!"

"I should say she did!" Pa exclaimed. "Where is this wolf?"

"I don't know. It is gone," Laura said.

Ma helped them take off their coats. "Sit down and rest," she said. "You are all out of breath."

"Where was the wolf?" Pa wanted to know.

"Up on the bank," Carrie said.

Laura nodded. "The high bank across the lake."

"Did you girls go clear there?" Pa asked in surprise. "And ran all the way back after you saw him! I had no idea you would go so far. It is a good half mile."

"We followed the moon path," Laura told him.

Pa looked at her strangely. "You would," he smiled. Then he grew serious. "I thought those wolves had gone. It was careless of me.

69

I'll hunt them tomorrow."

Mary's face was white. "Oh, girls!" she whispered. "Suppose he had caught you."

They were all silent.

Laura was glad to be safe in the warm room. If anything had happened to Carrie, it would have been her fault.

But nothing had happened. She thought of the great wolf with the wind ruffling the moonlight on his fur.

"Pa!" she said in a low voice.

"Yes, Laura?"

"I hope you don't ever find the wolf," Laura said.

"Why ever not?" asked Ma.

"Because he didn't chase us," Laura told her. "He didn't chase us, Pa, and he could have caught us."

Outside, a long, wild wolf howl rose and faded away.

If you're done with your chores,
have fun with these

activities!

MEET LAURA

Laura Ingalls Wilder was born in the Big Woods of Wisconsin on February 7, 1867, to Charles Ingalls and his wife, Caroline.

When Laura was still a baby, Pa and Ma decided to move to a farm near Keytesville, Missouri, and the family lived there about a year. Then they moved to land on the prairie south of Independence, Kansas. After two years in their little house on the prairie, the Ingallses went back to the Big Woods to live in the same house they had left three years earlier.

This time the family remained in the Big Woods for three years. These were the years that Laura wrote about in her first book, *Little House in the Big Woods*.

In the winter of 1874, when Laura was seven, Ma and Pa decided to move west to Minnesota. They found a beautiful farm near Walnut Grove, on the banks of Plum Creek.

The next two years were hard ones for the Ingallses. Swarms of grasshoppers devoured all the crops in the area, and Ma and Pa could not pay off all their debts. The family decided they could no longer keep the farm on Plum Creek, so they moved to Burr Oak, Iowa.

After a year in Iowa, the family returned to Walnut Grove again, and Pa built a house in town and started a butcher shop. Laura was ten years old by then, and she helped earn money for the family by working in the dining room of the hotel in Walnut Grove, babysitting, and running errands.

The family moved only once more, to the little town of De Smet in Dakota Territory. Laura was now twelve and had lived in at least twelve little houses. Laura grew into a young lady in De Smet, and met her husband, Almanzo Wilder, there.

Laura and Almanzo were married in 1885, and their daughter, Rose, was born in December 1886. By the spring of 1890, Laura and Almanzo had endured too many hardships to continue farming in South Dakota. Their house had burned down in 1889, and their second child, a boy, had died before he was a month old.

First, Laura, Almanzo, and Rose went east to Spring Valley, Minnesota, to live with Almanzo's family. About a year later they moved south to Florida. But Laura did not like Florida, and the family returned to De Smet.

In 1894, Laura, Almanzo, and Rose left De Smet for good and settled in Mansfield, Missouri.

When Laura was in her fifties, she began to write down her memories of her childhood, and in 1932, when Laura was 65 years old, *Little House in the Big Woods* was published. It was an immediate success, and Laura was asked to write more books about her life on the frontier.

Laura died on February 10, 1957, three days after her ninetieth birthday, but interest in the Little House books continued to grow. Since their first publication so many years ago, the Little House books have been read by millions of readers all over the world.

The Little House Family Tree

MARTHA ——♥——— LEWIS TUCKER
(1782–1862)

LEWIS   LYDIA   THOMAS   CHARLOTTE   MARY
(b. 1802)   (b. 1805)   (b. 1807)   (1809–1884)   (b. 1813)

♥——— HENRY QUINER
(1807–1844)

JOSEPH   HENRY   MARTHA   CAROLINE   ELIZA   THOMAS
(1834–1862)   (1835–1882)   (1837–1927)   (1839–1924)   (1842–1931)   (1844–1903)

♥——— CHARLES INGALLS
(1836–1902)

MARY   LAURA   CAROLINA (CARRIE)   GRACE
(1865–1928)   (1867–1957)   (1870–1946)   (1877–1941)

♥——— ALMANZO WILDER
(1857–1949)

ROSE
(1886–1968)

79

WORD SCRAMBLE

Unscramble the following words from *Animal Adventures*!

LBODLUG

SEOFX

ESVLOW

SNUSA

TPARENH

LGLFITANH

RSFU

YEUKS

BNRYRAAD

VBARE

IGNCDAN

AGRNPAD

TRPETEO

HSYAGG

EROTSIS

SIUMC

INNOSVE

WAHOSDS

EOARTDEMSEH

OGNILTHMO

WORD SEARCH

Find the following words from *Animal Adventures* in the puzzle below!

CAMPFIRE	BEAR	PROMISE
CORNCAKES	LONGHORN	GHOST
BUFFALO	GALLOP	STITCHES
ATTENTION	JACKRABBIT	RAILROAD
DEER	COWBOY	BUGGY
CLAWS	BADGER	FLANNEL
LEADER	JUICY	

```
S A B D B A D G E R X G A
P R O M I S E C W D E C T
Z H C A M P F I R E F K T
G A L L O P V D K E G Y E
F E A I L E A D E R I S N
C G W C D T C A R H D T T
O B S K U B O Q S E L I I
W U M B E A R J C F O T O
B G H O S T N P H M N C N
O G G F B L C A M N G H O
Y Y B U F F A L O A H E E
H C J D F G K L D N O S J
C A M P F I E Y H K R Z U
J B A M I G S F J L N B I
H E B R A I L R O A D L C
X J A C K R A B B I T K Y
C I D X E A F L A N N E L
```

ANSWER KEY

Word Scramble:

BULLDOG	BARNYARD
FOXES	BRAVE
WOLVES	DANCING
SUSAN	GRANDPA
PANTHER	TREETOP
NIGHTFALL	SHAGGY
FURS	STORIES
SUKEY	MUSIC

VENISON   HOMESTEADER

SHADOWS   MOONLIGHT

Word Search:

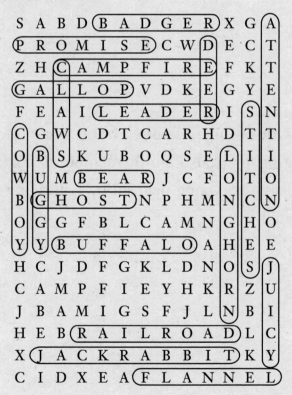

```
S A B D B A D G E R X G A
P R O M I S E C W D E C T
Z H C A M P F I R E F K T
G A L L O P V D K E G Y E
F E A I L E A D E R I S N
C G W C D T C A R H D T T
O B S K U B O Q S E L I I
W U M B E A R J C F O T O
B G H O S T N P H M N C N
O G G F B L C A M N G H O
Y Y B U F F A L O A H E E
H C J D F G K L D N O S J
C A M P F I E Y H K R Z U
J B A M I G S F J L N B I
H E B R A I L R O A D L C
X J A C K R A B B I T K Y
C I D X E A F L A N N E L
```

SING-ALONG

One of Ingalls family's favorite activities is singing. So grab a family member or a friend and sing this song beloved by Laura and her family!

"Pop! Goes the Weasel"

Words Traditional USA

That night, for a special birthday treat, Pa played "Pop Goes the Weasel" for Laura. He sat with Laura and Mary close against his knees while he played. "Now watch," he said. "Watch, and maybe you can see the weasel pop out this time."

A penny for a spool of thread,
Another for a needle,
That's the way the money goes—
Pop! goes the weasel!

All around the cobbler's bench,

The monkey chased the weasel,
The preacher kissed the cobbler's wife—
Pop! goes the weasel!
Potatoes for an Irishman's taste,
A doctor for the measles,
A fiddler always for a dance—
Pop! goes the weasel!
Blood pudding for a Dutchman's meal,
A workman for a chisel,
The preacher kissed the cobbler's wife—
Pop! goes the weasel!

From round about the countrymen's barn
The mice began to mizzle,
For when they poke their noses out—
Pop! goes the weasel!
The painter works with ladder and brush,
The artist with the easel,
The fiddler always snaps the strings at—
Pop! goes the weasel!

DESIGN YOUR OWN LITTLE HOUSE

The house that Pa built for the family on the prairie was only thirteen feet wide by seventeen feet long. That's the size of just one room in many houses today! Laura describes the house as being set up like this:

If you were designing your own little house, how would you arrange it? Think about all that would need to fit—beds for everyone, kitchen supplies, a table, chairs, and so on—and draw a floor plan like Laura's to show what you would do.

Laura and her sisters may live in a little house, but they're always ready for big adventure. Don't miss:

LAURA &
NELLIE

LITTLE HOUSE CHAPTER BOOK #4

CHAPTER 1
COUNTRY GIRLS

Laura Ingalls never forgot the first time she met Nellie Oleson. It was on Laura's first day of school, when she lived in Minnesota.

Laura and her big sister, Mary, and her little sister, Carrie, lived on a farm with their Ma and Pa and their bulldog, Jack. Living on a farm meant Laura was a country girl.

Laura loved being a country girl. She loved to run out of the house in the morning and see the dew sparkling on the prairie grass.

She loved to wade in the creek where the minnows swam. She loved to poke a stick at the old crab who lived in the creek and watch him come out snapping his sharp claws. She loved the good smells of hay and earth and wind.

Nellie Oleson was not a country girl. She was a town girl.

When Nellie Oleson first saw Laura, she wrinkled up her nose as though she smelled something bad. She didn't—she was just being snooty. Nellie's father owned a store, and Nellie thought that made her very important.

"Hmph!" sniffed Nellie Oleson, looking Laura and Mary up and down. She looked at their faded dresses and their long legs sticking out from under the hems. She looked at their braids, tied with thread.

"Country girls!" she said.

Laura didn't much like Nellie Oleson,

even if she did have pretty yellow curls tied with big blue ribbons. Nellie's dress was store-bought. It was smooth and white, with little blue flowers all over. Nellie wore shiny black shoes, and her dress was as light and delicate as a spring day. She was pretty as a picture, except for that wrinkled-up nose.

Laura and Mary were barefoot. When the weather was warm, they always went barefoot. They loved the feel of the soft grass and warm dirt beneath their feet. Ma made all their clothes. She bought sturdy red calico for Laura's dresses, and sturdy blue calico for Mary's. Laura and Mary had never had a white dress like Nellie's.

But Laura and Mary were too busy that first day of school to worry much about Nellie Oleson. They had never been to school before, even though Laura was almost eight and Mary was going on nine. Until now, the places they had lived in had been too far away from any town for them to go to school.

They were excited to meet their teacher, Miss Beadle. She left them inside the one-room schoolhouse and showed them where to sit.

Ma had given Laura and Mary a book to study from. But they did not have a slate.

"I will lend you mine," Teacher said. "You cannot learn to write without a slate."

She lifted up the top of her desk and took out a piece of black board. That was the slate. There was a piece of chalk, too, to write on the slate with.

At noon, all the other children went home to eat. Laura and Mary's house on the farm was two and a half miles away. That was too long a walk to go home for dinner. So Laura and Mary took their dinner pail and sat in a shady spot against the schoolhouse. They ate their bread and butter and talked.

"I like school," Mary said.

"So do I," said Laura. "But I don't like that Nellie Oleson that called us country girls."

"We are country girls," Mary pointed out.

"Yes," Laura said proudly. "She needn't wrinkle her nose!"

CHAPTER 2
TOWN GIRL

The very next day, Laura and Mary had to go to Nellie's father's store. Pa had given them a nickel to buy a slate of their own. They must not go on borrowing Teacher's slate, he said.

The morning sun was shining brightly when they climbed the steps of Mr. Oleson's store. Laura blinked a little inside the cool shady building.

A man stood behind the counter. Laura guessed that was Mr. Oleson, the shopkeeper.

She looked around at all the wonderful things on the shelves—pails and pickles and ploughs and a large round yellow cheese. There were dozens of interesting things for sale. Laura would have liked to look at them all.

But suddenly the back door slammed open. In flounced Nellie Oleson. She looked right at Laura and Mary, standing in the doorway in their bare feet.

"Yah! Yah!" shouted a little boy behind Nellie. He was her brother, Willie, and he had teased Laura and Mary at school the day before. He had called them snipes because their dresses were too short. Snipes were birds with funny long legs, and Laura and Mary did look a little like snipes with their legs sticking out beneath the hems of their dresses. But it wasn't nice to be reminded of it.

"Yah! Long-legged snipes!" Willie jeered now.

"Shut up, Willie," said Mr. Oleson.

But Willie did not shut up. He went on saying, "Snipes! Snipes!"

With a little smile on her face, Nellie walked right past Mary and Laura to a tall wooden barrel that stood on the floor. She dug her hands into the pail and came up with two fistfuls of candy.

It was Christmas candy. There were striped pieces, round pieces, pieces like ribbons. There was red and green and white candy. It was beautiful! Nellie stared right at Laura and Mary, as she crammed the beautiful candies into her mouth.

Willie laughed, and grabbed a handful of candy for himself. He shoveled it into his mouth. Neither one of them offered any to Laura or Mary. Not a single piece.

"Nellie! You and Willie go right back out of here!" Mr. Oleson said.

But Nellie and Willie ignored him. *Crunch, crunch* went the candy in their mouths. They kept on staring at Mary and Laura.

Mary turned away from them. She told Mr. Oleson she needed a slate and handed him Pa's nickel.

Mr. Oleson gave her the slate. "You'll want a slate pencil, too," he said. "Here it is. One penny."

"They haven't got a penny," Nellie said.

"Well, take it along, and tell your Pa to give me the penny next time he comes to town," said Mr. Oleson.

But Mary said, "No, sir. Thank you." She turned around and so did Laura, and they walked out of the store.

At the door Laura looked back. Nellie made a face at her. Nellie's tongue was streaked red and green from the candy.

Laura and Mary were quiet as they walked

to the schoolhouse. Laura was worried about the slate pencil they needed to buy. She hated to ask Pa for another penny, after he had spent so much on the slate. Then she remembered their Christmas pennies. One year, back in Indian Territory, they had each found a penny in their Christmas stockings. They could use those pennies for slate pencils. And they would buy the pencils at Mr. Beadle's store, not at Mr. Oleson's.

That made Laura feel better. But she kept thinking about Nellie sticking out her red-and-green tongue.

Mary was still thinking about Nellie, too. "My goodness!" she said. "I couldn't be as mean as that Nellie Oleson."

I could, Laura thought. I could be meaner to her than she is to us, if Ma and Pa would let me.

The definitive full-color guide to the Little House series

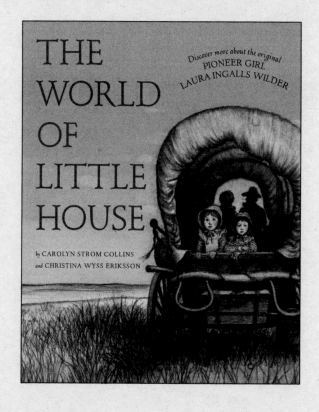

THE WORLD OF LITTLE HOUSE

Discover more about the original PIONEER GIRL LAURA INGALLS WILDER

by CAROLYN STROM COLLINS
and CHRISTINA WYSS ERIKSSON

Featuring authentic photographs, maps, crafts, and recipes and a detailed exploration of how each of the beloved Little House books is connected to Laura's own pioneer days

---

HARPER
An Imprint of HarperCollinsPublishers

www.littlehousebooks.com

Little House for Younger Readers

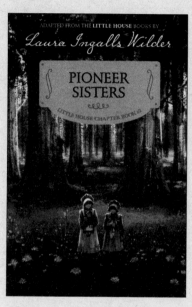

Grand adventures await in the Little House chapter books,
adapted from Laura Ingalls Wilder's beloved classics

HARPER
An Imprint of HarperCollinsPublishers

www.littlehousebooks.com